the
TEMPEST

FAMILIUS

Published by Familius LLC, www.familius.com
Familius books are available at special discounts for bulk purchases
for sales promotions or for family or corporate use. Special
editions, including personalized covers, excerpts of existing books,
or books with corporate logos, can be created in large quantities
for special needs. For more information, contact Premium Sales at
559-876-2170 or email specialmarkets@familius.com.

Originally published by Sweet Cherry Publishing, Ltd, 2013
Text & illustration by Macaw Books, 2013

Library of Congress Catalog-in-Publication Data
2015942872
ISBN 9781942934318

Printed in the United States of America

Edited by Michele Robbins
Cover design by David Miles

10 9 8 7 6 5 4 3 2 1

First Edition

About
SHAKESPEARE

William Shakespeare, regarded as the greatest writer in the English language, was born in Stratford-upon-Avon in Warwickshire, England (around April 23, 1564). He was the third of eight children born to John and Mary Shakespeare.

Shakespeare was a poet, playwright, and dramatist. He is often known as England's national poet and the "Bard of Avon." Thirty-eight plays, 154 sonnets, two long narrative poems, and several other poems are attributed to him. Shakespeare's plays have been translated into every major language and are performed more often than those of any other playwright.

MAIN CHARACTERS

Prospero is the play's protagonist. He was the Duke of Milan until his brother plotted against him and usurped him. He has spent twelve years marooned on an island with his daughter, Miranda.

Miranda is Prospero's daughter. She is compassionate, loyal to her father, and nonjudgmental.

Ferdinand is the son of the King of Naples. He falls in love with Miranda when he first sees her.

Ariel is a supernatural being, a spirit. He is mischievous, powerful, and does all that Prospero asks of him.

THE TEMPEST

Prospero, the Duke of Milan, was a learned man who lived among his books, leaving the management of his dukedom to his brother, Antonio, in whom he had complete trust.

But Antonio wanted to become the duke himself and plotted his brother's death.

With the help of Prospero's enemy, Alonso, the King of Naples, Antonio managed to get what he wanted. They took Prospero to sea, and when they were far away from land, they forced him into a little boat with no tackle, mast, or sail. They put his little daughter, Miranda (not yet three years old), into the boat with

him and sailed away, leaving them to their fate. So, in this treacherous manner, Antonio usurped the dukedom of Milan.

But one among the courtiers, Lord Gonzalo, was true to his rightful master, Prospero. He secretly placed some fresh water,

provisions, and clothes in the
boat, along with what Prospero
valued most of all—some of his
precious books. After a rough
ride at sea for several days, the
boat finally reached an island,
and Prospero and his little
daughter disembarked safely.

This island was enchanted. For years it had been under the spell of a wicked witch Sycorax, who had imprisoned all the good spirits in the trunks of trees. She died shortly before Prospero was cast on the shores, but the spirits, the chief of whom was called Ariel, still remained imprisoned.

Now, Prospero was a great magician. He had devoted himself to the study of magic over the years while his brother had managed the affairs of Milan. By using his magic,

he set free the imprisoned spirits,
yet he kept them obedient to
his will. Prospero treated them
kindly as long as they did his
bidding, and he exercised his
power over them wisely.

There was one creature,
though, whom Prospero found

it necessary to treat with
harshness—this was Caliban,
the son of the wicked witch.
He was a hideous,
deformed monster,
vicious and
brutal in nature.
Caliban, whom

Prospero taught to speak, did not want to learn anything good or useful and was therefore employed as a slave to fetch wood and do all the laborious work; and Ariel had the responsibility of compelling

him to do these services. The
lively little Ariel had nothing
mischievous in his nature,
except that he took pleasure
in tormenting Caliban. When
Caliban was lazy and neglected
his work, Ariel (who was

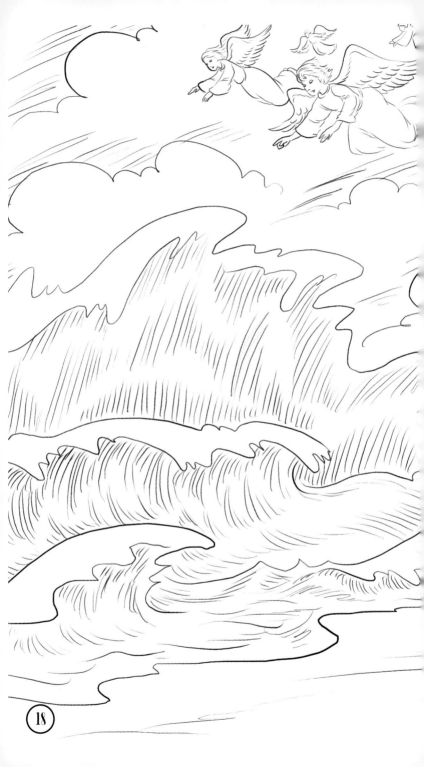

invisible to all except Prospero)
would pinch him and sometimes
make him trip and fall.

    With the powerful spirits
obedient to his will, Prospero
could, by their means, command
the winds and the waves of the sea.

Years went by, and Miranda
grew up into a young girl,
sweet and fair. One day, when
Miranda was about fifteen
years old, it so happened that
Antonio, Prospero's false brother,
and Alonso, the king, with

Sebastian, Alonso's brother, and
Ferdinand, Alonso's son, were at
sea together with Lord Gonzalo,
and their ship came near
Prospero's island. Seeing this,
Prospero gave orders to the
spirits to raise a violent storm.

While the tempest was raging, Prospero showed his daughter the big ship trying to fight the waves and told her that it was filled with living human beings like themselves. Miranda, feeling sad for them, requested that her father stop what he was doing. Prospero told her that he intended to

save every one of them. Then, for the first time, he told her the story of his life, and that he had caused this storm to rise so that his enemies, Antonio and Alonso, who were onboard, would be delivered into his hands.

Ending the story, Prospero gently touched his daughter with his magic wand, and she fell fast asleep.

Ariel, the spirit, had just then presented himself before his master to give an account of the tempest. The spirits were always invisible to Miranda, but even so, Prospero did not like to talk to them in his daughter's presence.

Ariel described the storm and how the king's son, Ferdinand, had been the first to leap into the sea, and how his father

11

thought his dear son had been swallowed up by the waves.

"But he is safe," said Ariel, "in a corner of the island, sitting sadly, lamenting the loss of his father, who he assumes to be drowned."

"Where are the king and my brother?" asked Prospero.

"I left them searching for Ferdinand," answered Ariel. "Of the ship's crew, no one is missing, though each one thinks himself to be the only one saved. And the ship is safe in the harbor."

"Well done, Ariel, but there is more work to be done yet," said Prospero. "Now bring the young prince here. My daughter must see him."

"More work?" exclaimed Ariel. "Let me remind you, master, you have promised me my freedom."

"I remember all," said Prospero. "But you do not seem to recollect what torment I freed you from. Have you forgotten how the wicked witch Sycorax imprisoned you in a tree?"

"Pardon me, dear master," said Ariel, ashamed at having appeared ungrateful. "I will obey your commands."

"Do so," said Prospero, "and I will set you free."

Away went Ariel, taking the form of a water nymph, to where he had left Ferdinand. Invisible to him, Ariel hovered nearby and began singing.

"Full fathom five thy father lies;
Of his bones are coral made.

Those are pearls that were his eyes;
Nothing of him that doth fade.
But doth suffer a sea change;
Into something rich and strange.
Sea nymphs hourly ring his knell.
Hark! Now I hear them,
ding dong bell!"

The news of
his lost father soon
roused the prince,
and he followed
the sound of Ariel's
voice until it led
him to Prospero and
Miranda, who were
sitting in the shade
of a large tree.

Then, everything
happened as Prospero
desired. Miranda,
who had not seen any
other human being
except her father for
as long as she could
remember, looked
at the youthful

prince with wonder in her eyes
and love in her heart. Ferdinand,
seeing such a lovely girl in this
deserted place, and after hearing
the strange song, thought he
was on an enchanted island and
that Miranda was its goddess.

But Prospero, though
secretly delighted, pretended to
be angry. "You have come here as
a spy," he shouted at Ferdinand.

"I will chain your neck and
feet together, and you shall
feed on freshwater mussels
and withered roots, and have
seawater to drink. Follow me."

"No," said Ferdinand, and
drew his sword.

But Prospero,
waving his magic
wand, fixed him to

the spot so that he stood as still as a stone statue.

In terror, Miranda requested that her father have mercy on the young prince, but Prospero refused to do so and made Ferdinand follow him to his cell. There he made the prince work hard, carrying heavy logs of timber and piling them up. Ferdinand patiently obeyed.

Miranda offered to help Ferdinand, but he refused; yet, he could not keep from

her the secret of his love, and she, upon hearing it, rejoiced and promised to be his wife. Hearing them profess their love for each other, Prospero released Ferdinand from his servitude and, glad at heart, gave his consent to their marriage.

Meanwhile, Antonio (brother of Prospero) and Sebastian (brother of King Alonso), on another part of the island, were plotting the murder of Alonso, the King of Naples. They had assumed Ferdinand to be dead, and felt that Sebastian would succeed to the throne upon

Alonso's death. They intended
to carry out their wicked plan
while their victim was asleep,
but Ariel woke him before
they had a chance to attack.

Ariel then set about his
usual tricks. He appeared
before them in the shape of a
harpy—a voracious monster

with wings—and the feast
vanished. Then, to their utter
amazement, the harpy spoke
to them, reminding them
of their cruelty in driving
Prospero from his dukedom
and leaving him and his
infant daughter to perish
at sea, saying that for this
reason they would suffer.

The King
of Naples and
Antonio repented
of the injustice
they had done to
Prospero, and Ariel told his
master that he was certain their
penitence was sincere.

"Then bring them here,
Ariel," said Prospero.

Ariel led the men, including faithful Gonzalo, to Prospero's tent. At first, no one except Gonzalo recognized Prospero.

Antonio, in tears and with words of sorrow and true repentance, implored his brother for forgiveness, and the king expressed his sincere remorse for having assisted Antonio in deposing his brother.

Prospero forgave them.

Once they had promised to restore his dukedom, Prospero said to the King of Naples, "I have a gift for you, too." Prospero drew back a curtain and showed him Ferdinand and Miranda playing chess. Alonso and his son were overjoyed to

greet each other again, for they
had each thought the other
had drowned in the storm.

The King of Naples was
almost as astonished by the
beauty and grace of the young
Miranda as his son had been.

"Who is this maid?" he asked. "She seems to be the goddess who has brought us together."

"No, sir," answered Ferdinand, amused to find that his father had made the same mistake as he had when he

first saw Miranda.
"She is a mortal, the
daughter of Prospero,
the real Duke of
Milan. I had heard much
about him, but never seen him
until now; I have received new

life from him. And he has become a second father to me, giving me this dear lady."

"Then I must ask for her forgiveness, too," said the king.

"No more of that," said Prospero. "Let us not remember

our past troubles, since they have ended so happily." And then he embraced his brother, assuring him of his forgiveness.

Prospero then told them that their ship was safe in the harbor, the sailors all onboard, and that he and his daughter

would accompany them
home the next morning.

"In the meantime," he said,
"enjoy as much refreshment
as you want; and for your
evening's entertainment, I will tell
you the story of my life from the
day I arrived on this desert island."

He then called for
Caliban to prepare some food
and set the cave in order.

Soon, all were filled as well
as forgiven. Safe from the sea
and seeing the budding love of

sweet Miranda and honorable Ferdinand, all were merry. So all ended happily. The next day, they set sail for Naples, where Ferdinand and Miranda were to be married. Ariel gave them calm seas and auspicious gales.

Prospero, after many years of absence, went back to his own dukedom, where he was welcomed with great joy by his faithful subjects. He stopped practicing the art of magic, and his life was happy, not only because he had found his own dukedom again, but because when his bitterest foes who had done him wrong lay at his mercy, he took no vengeance on them but nobly forgave them.

As for Ariel, Prospero set him free so that he could wander where he wished and sing with a light heart his sweet song:

"Where the bee sucks, there suck I:
In a cowslip's bell I lie;
There I couch when owls do cry.
On the bat's back I do fly
After summer, merrily:
Merrily, merrily, shall I live now,
Under the blossom that
hangs on the bough."

Prospero, the Duke of Milan, is robbed of his title and marooned on a deserted island with his beautiful daughter, Miranda. Using magic, he calls upon the powerful spirits of the island to help him reclaim his old life and face those who wronged him. When a handsome prince falls in love with Miranda, Prospero must choose whether to take revenge on his usurpers or forgive them.

A tale of magic and monsters and shipwrecks, *The Tempest* reads almost like a fairy tale. This classic Shakespeare play was one of the very last the Bard wrote and covers very deep and important themes of power, love, and redemption.

WILLIAM SHAKESPEARE (1564-1616)

Playwright. Poet. Actor. Producer. Legend. William Shakespeare is widely regarded as one of the greatest writers in the English language, and his work has influenced centuries of writers and thinkers. His collected works—from plays to poems—have been translated into every language and are performed to the delight of audiences the world over.

ISBN 978-1-942934-31-8

9 781942 934318

5 0 6 9 5 >

HELPING FAMILIES BE HAPPY

Visit us at www.familius.com for books, articles, and videos to help your family be happy.